MW01166686

Minerals

Sy Barlowe

DOVER PUBLICATIONS, INC.
Mineola, New York

Bibliographical Note

Learning About Minerals is a new work, first published by Dover
Publications, Inc., in 1998.

International Standard Book Number: 0-486-40017-4

Manufactured in the United States of America
Dover Publications, Inc., 31 East 2nd Street, Mineola, N.Y. 11501

Introduction

Minerals are the materials that make up the earth's top layer. They are stony mixtures of one or more natural elements that people find within rocks. Minerals have become main ingredients in things we use everyday, such as pencils, glasses, and thermometers. The stickers in this book illustrate twelve different minerals. As you place them on the appropriate pages you will learn where they come from and how they are used. Collecting rocks and minerals is so much fun, you may want to start your own collection!

Quartz

Quartz is one of the most common minerals found in earth's crust. Usually white or colorless, quartz may be brown, black, yellow, pink, green, or blue. Considered a semi-precious gem, quartz has been used in jewelry since the Middle Ages. Glass is made from quartz sand. Quartz crystals have been used in radios, televisions, and lenses. Often found in limestone caves, quartz occurs in Brazil, Scotland, and the United States.

Feldspar

Feldspar, the most abundant of all mineral groups, is created deep in the earth. One of the most familiar varieties is Labradorite, shown here, a feldspar that sparkles with an iridescent blue and green. Considered a gem by collectors, labradorite is found in Laborador, Newfoundland.

Fluorite

Fluorite is fun to collect because its beautiful crystal fragments come in a variety of colors including white, blue, green, and violet. Sometimes translucent, fluorite may show a fluorescent glow under an ultraviolet light. Fluorite is used in making steel, ore, gasoline, and freon for refrigeration. Most of the world's fluorite is mined in Illinois, Kentucky, Colorado, and New Mexico.

Galena

Lead has been extracted from galena since ancient times. The Romans made water pipes from it, and when the printing press was invented, galena was the base of the metal used for type. Although the largest deposits of this silver-colored mineral occur in the United States, galena is also found in Europe, South America, and Australia.

Mica

Mica can be peeled into paper-thin, flexible sheets. The most common mica is muscovite, named after Moscow, where it was first used as a substitute for glass windows. Usually colorless, muscovite can also be gray, brown, light green, lavender, or ruby red. It is found in South Dakota, but the most perfect muscovite is mined in India.

Malachite

Malachite, often found together with blue azurite, is cut and polished to enhance its striking pattern of light and dark green bands. Crafted into amulets and bracelets by ancient people who believed it protected them from disease, lightning, and witchcraft, today malachite is set into jewelry. Found in England, Africa, and Arizona, the finest malachite is mined in Russia.

Pyrite

Pyrite looks so much like gold it is often called "fool's gold." From the Greek word *pyr*, meaning fire, pyrite is named for the sparks that fly when it is struck by a hammer. The Incas polished slabs of pyrite to make mirrors. Ancient people crafted pyrite into ornaments; today it is used in costume jewelry. Pyrite is found in Spain, Japan, the United States, Canada, and other countries.

Talc

Because it's the world's softest mineral, you can easily scratch talc with your fingernail. Ancient Chinese and Native American Indians carved soapstone, a form of talc, into decorative objects. Talc is used today in powder, rubber, porcelain, and insecticides. White or apple green in color, talc is found along mountain lines in the United States, Austria, and other countries.

Graphite

Coming from the Greek word meaning "to write," graphite is best known for its use as pencil lead. A soft, gray-colored mineral, it is mixed with other materials to make it harder. It is also used in the electrical and chemical industries. While there are graphite mines in the United States, the richest deposits of graphite are in Korea, Sri Lanka, Mexico, and Madagascar.

Azurite

Azurite is a favorite among collectors because of its deep-blue crystals. Often found together with malachite, azurite is much more rare. Considered a semi-precious stone, azurite is unearthed in copper mining areas throughout the world including Arizona in the United States, and Namibia in South West Africa. The most perfect pieces of azurite come from France.

Cinnabar

Cinnabar, from which mercury is extracted, was mined by ancient Romans; some of these mines are still in use. With color that runs from black to bright red, cinnabar was used by early Greeks as a red pigment. Found near hot springs and volcanic rocks in America and Spain, cinnabar is used in thermometers, explosives, and in the chemical industry.

Calcite

Calcite-rich drip stone accumulates on the rock surfaces of caverns; it hangs from ceilings as stalactites and rises from floors as stalagmites. Limestone, formed mainly from calcite, makes up most shells and many fossils. Iceland spar, a calcite, is used in microscopes because it can split beams of light. Calcite can be colorless, opaque or tinted light red, yellow, or brown. It is found in South Dakota and England.